“In this vital new collection of poems by Ash Good,
desire for the sacred, desire for oneness with the Beloved,
becomes a journey and a story. This journey/story begins
with visionary observations such as ‘the universe fits in
that two-man tent,’ and concludes with the epiphany-like
acknowledgment of ‘the gauze/of the thing/that connects
everything.’ Here, inner life and outward existence—spirit
and body—are both given their due in a voice as spare and
natural as Gary Snyder’s, as insightful and alchemical as
Rumi’s. Open *These Things Will Never Happen Quite Like
That Again*, read it cover to cover, and enter the sacred
and sensuous space created by this gifted poet. You
will want to reside there.”

—GAIL WRONSKY, AUTHOR OF *SO QUICK BRIGHT THINGS*

Years Grew a Keloid

LETTERSAT
3AMPRESS

THESE THINGS WILL NEVER HAPPEN QUITE LIKE THAT AGAIN

—

ASH GOOD

Paperback ISBN: 978-0-9974436-2-2
Library of Congress Control Number: 2017935495

Published in 2017 by LettersAt3amPress
Box 93 Meadow Vista, CA 95722
editor@3amproductions.org
Publisher/Editors: Jazmin Aminian Jordán, Michael Ventura
Editor-At-Large: Rebekah J. Morton
Social Media Manager: Ashley C. Aminian

LETTERSAT3AMPRESS.ORG

For these dear ones
who grow my heart—
who I adventure here
with in matter.

PUBLISHER'S PREFACE

————

*These Things Will Never Happen Quite Like
That Again* is a read-in-one-sitting kind of book—
and then you read it again to see where you've
been. It's not a poem, except when it is. It's too
impressionistic to be called a memoir—but aren't
impressions all we have? It's not a story—or is it?
What it *is* is: a word-being that refuses classification.
It couldn't care less what you call it; in fact, by the
end, you may be more concerned about what *it*
calls *you*. A critic might call it experimental but I
call it a voice, utterly alive, tough, lyrical, concrete
always, sensual always—a voice telling us, from the
title on, truths as basic and vital as *These Things
Will Never Happen Quite Like That Again.*

—Michael Ventura, February 2017

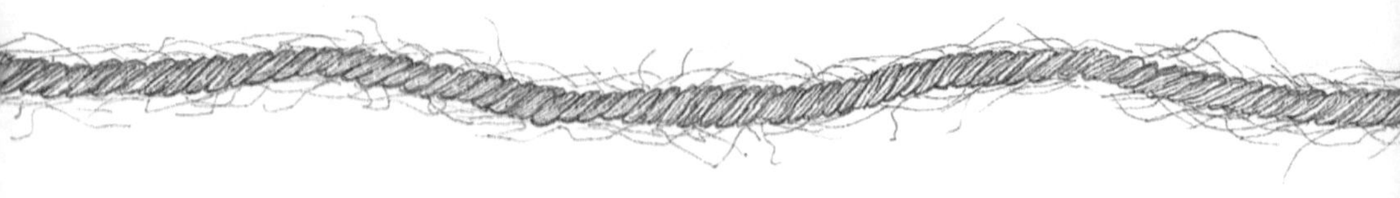

Right now, today,
we are still alive,
and our bodies are
working marvelously.
Our eyes can still
see the beautiful sky.
Our ears can still
hear…our loved ones.

—*Thich Nhat Hanh*

I AM BORN
IN PARADISE

California, at a time I can never remember,
      on the seventh hot day of July in 1984.

My mama is alone at the hospital
      until Aunt Sharel gets there fresh
from decorating a wedding cake.

Then it's just me and mama until over a year later
      when she marries a handsome young
fireman from a tiny town in Oregon
      who's been wooing her since summers before.

Gramp says
      I remember the first day I saw you—
      curled up sleeping on my living room floor,
      right there in front of the daveneau.

He must think his young son is crazy—with this girl
        from Cali-fornia-way and a precocious blonde
baby that isn't his—but if he does,
        I never know.

My childhood is filled with pilgrimages
        to my mama's homeland—where I ride
in the back of a rusty farm truck
        (with no seat belts, don't tell daddy)
from the old Mexican restaurant mama's family likes,
        smelling the hot summer hay and watching
the sky burn up in a million colors until
        the stars stop being shy.

In the eighties my daddy has a mullet,
        permed down to his collar, and
my mama's bangs feather
        like a country music star.

On rare nights they get pretty and she smells
        like *Laura Ashley* and I pretend to sleep
at Gran and Gramp's—crying
        (while I'm sure they're in a car wreck dying)
until it's late when they pick me up.

FIRST I
REMEMBER

My mattress is on the floor and the window
is high on the wall and at night

       trees from the ravine
       (who knows what lives down there?)
       throw long stalking shapes

on the paint.

I stay still and watch endless and worry about

              what is coming.

Maybe I am fifteen months old?

But in the morning mama puts me in Osh'kosh.

I pick dandelions from sidewalk cracks.

      Grandpa Dell (who isn't really my grandpa)
      comes from across the street.

He takes my hand and
we pull a carrot from his garden.

      I hold it from its leafy green
      top while he sprays it off.

      Warm hose water,
      the smell of dirt
      and an earthy orange crunch

            is enough
            to forget

                  the shadows
                  I see.

THE SCANNER IS ALWAYS BEEPING LOUD

Me and Jeffy play at Gran and Gramp's.

We hide in the small circle of hallway
and pretend to be like daddy with our siren cars
and fire trucks.

The scanner is always beeping loud as ambulances
and policemen get called around town.

I'm dispatch and Jeffy drives the rescue when
a loud crack comes from the pane window
in the living room.

We run out and a car is flipped on its side,
between the fence next door and a tree and a man
is on the ground a few feet away and the whole
thing is on fire and
our toy rescues aren't much help.

I STRUGGLE
TO ESCAPE

———

My great uncle wears heavy Romeos.
           Brown leather I put baby feet in.
Gramp and Gran and Cousin Don
      all call him Cleaver.
        I'm not sure why.
He calls my great aunt Kuni (on account
      of Kuni BMW over in Tigard).
He calls me prune picker since me
      and mama come here from California.

His club chair is studded with bronze rivets,
     diamond patterned, in the corner of the den.
He sits next to the magazine stand and
     under the black and white photo of him and
       Cousin Don swept up in windy dunes.
Me and Jeffy crawl between those boots
     and giggle hard when his voice growls
      TRASH COMPACTOR.

He squeezes against me, big knobby
        knees under rough slacks, and shakes
            and shakes.
I struggle to escape
        and crawl away red faced,
            then return eager for my turn again.
Daddy now, don't be so rough
                to those kids Kuni says.

I take walks with him down
        Matzen Street along the oak
            covered path to my grade school
        where we jump up and down
            on the wooden suspension bridge.

I'm in the back of his truck while
        he is trimming down vines
            from around power lines.
It's my seventh birthday when
        he twists to throw the branch
            and falls high from that ladder
                in front of me.

LEARNING
WINTER

———

I get big
in the drafty green farmhouse my daddy
grows up in, built by the farmer
who owns it before them.

I can see my breath when
I go down counting stairs (there are thirteen).

I turn on the oil heat and park my feet on the floor
vent—my ritual every early school morning.

But in high school I only have one pair of jeans so
in between turning the thermosat on and going to
burn myself on hot air, I put my clothes in the dryer.

One frosty Saturday I'm alone with house creaks
while mama and daddy and Jeffy sleep.

I pack my camera and pull the beat old Jag
I drive then out of the steep gravel onto Pittsburg.

I slip far out into country on black-ice roads
until a field of icicles calls to me.

I freeze them again frame by frame
then think I'd better get home
while everyone still sleeps.

TO LEAVE
I HAVE TO TAKE THE FREEWAY

The Duncan Trussel Family Hour whines
from door speakers as our 245DL blunders
over the under-maintained freeway that
tunnels through the parts of Los Angeles
where you really hope your car doesn't
break down—

Like that one time years ago, weeks after
we met, when Chronos' chain slips off,
stranding him in the bowels of the 110 until
a highway patrol officer begrudgingly lends
a prybar from his black and white (wary
of lawsuits and breaking policy).

Chronos manages to finagle the links back
on and later that night after I drink far too
much wine and smoke cannabis for the
third time I teeter on the top step outside.

He kisses my forehead and tells me
he loves me for the first time and to
go back inside. *These concrete stairs
aren't for drunk people.*

THESE DAYS

———

I finally get an invoice paid just before the first
and I walk down La Tijera, past the Jungle Video
and the 99 Cents and More and go to Chase first
to deposit a check in my account and go to Wells
Fargo next to give it all away to my landlord.

Chronos walks with me and maybe we'll go
to the Safeway after to buy GT Dave's or stop at
the liquor store for a lighter; anywhere as long
as we don't spend more than ten dollars.

We wander through mid-century homes on hygienic,
climate-controlled streets and overlook the bird
nest that lives in the sign at the corner of Kittyhawk
and Glascow until the day we do see it and wonder
if we've been paying attention to anything.

We break into the freeway trench and plod in
nuclear algae and scramble back up the rocks under
the overpass. He has sure footing and offers me a
hand. There's a pair of turquoise warehouse doors
where we stand in front to take a picture. His mullet
and my rat tail peddle the same irony but he's lean
and straight everywhere I spring up and curve.

When we fight I walk alone the two miles down
Centinela to get to Howard Hugh's where I sit
in the middle of an empty theatre and watch
The Lion King on special feature for its twentieth
anniversary. I head back near dusk and wonder then
if this is really such a good idea. *Hakuna Matata.*

I Google how to pack my first bowl and eat acid on
a torn shred of index card and climb up on the fourth
floor roof where the playa and LAX stretch to the
Pacific and I might just be an extra in *Blade Runner.*
Gravity speaks to me with no intermediary and
teaches me what yoga is while I ache for days far
out there (not knowing how much I'll miss these).

"MY GREATER SELF ROSE BEFORE ME"[†]

Once you hit the windmills, you're finally out
of Los Angeles. Well into the desert, well on
your way to nowhere.

We ride the Guzzi there, geared up, a heavy sail
of a pack on my back. The winds blow wild
across the highway and our bike floats,
leaned at forty degrees, skipping
from one side of a lane to another.

The yellow lines go straight until they disappear
past the earth's curve. My abs ache when
we roll up to Joshua Tree alongside
a 'round-the-world-traveler from Spain.
His Kawasaki's hardbags are covered
in sticker souvenirs of lands his two wheels
have already conquered.

Chronos makes friends fast.
We share a site, setting our tent high
up in boulders next to a desert bush
of honey flowers.

I make dinner over fire and later we try
to explain when we offer him a brownie—
They're special brownies. You know, like, weed?
He shakes his head and takes a bite of half of one.
Like, magic brownies? Cannabis?
He knows that word.
His eyes grow wide and he spits the second half out.
What will happen?
Chronos howls hysterically.
You'll get a real good night's sleep.

In the morning I rise
and Chronos has run off
to run up rocks
and our Spaniard companion is
still quiet in his tent.

I look at the glass pipe that smells like burning
tires, I look at the little crystals tawny and tacky
in the bag. Have you ever smoked this stuff
they make from an acacia tree?

I lay down inside and before I'm done
inhaling she starts dancing above me.
The universe fits in that two-man tent
while she's a queen hypnotizing
the creosote's bees.

Their vibrations fuel
the sole sound wave of being.
The quiet realizing happens
that I'm watching god,
that I'm watching me.

† With gratitude to Lucille Clifton's *it was a dream*

WHITE LIGHTS STARBURST
IN MY BAD NIGHT VISION

We drive in navy through the bad cow
part where the methane scrunches
Chronos' nose. When he gets out to pump
eighty-seven it's two in the morning and
I watch him, sleepy in the side mirror,
rest his head on the wagon's drip rail,
hand still on the nozzle.

The 76 station's bright white lights
starburst in my bad night vision.
The air halts heavy on my arm like
an unwanted heat blanket I wanna peel
back—the itchy blue one I kick off
Gran's spare bed.

The bristle on his face is short and
amber-tinted until it grows bushier and
red (even though his hair isn't).
Chronos gets noticed on a sidewalk
as that hipster Portland beard model
he is once
in a glossy Japanese magazine
and he trims it all off again.

THE FRAYS
ARE UNKNOTTED

———

*The trick is in
what one emphasizes.*

—Carlos Casteñeda

Fortunately when Chronos floors the
gas on our old blue Volvo to blast through
a real deep puddle on the way to a secret
beach, the water spray makes rainbows.
The road is hard dirt, sometimes muddy,
sometimes full of bumpy roots as it twists
and tumbles steep toward the shore.
The trees bolt up lush and lanky
and light flitters through leaves and lands
white on my thighs.

Unfortunately the engine quits when we're
seven miles down this rutted single lane.
The beach is right there but I'm busy calculating
the costs of being rescued from being stranded.
Chronos plays Whac-A-Mole with car gremlins.
Hunched under the hood, his indigo tank rings
salmon around the neck and those slight but
sinewed shoulders. A long angry scar from the
worst moto accident runs the length of the
bicep on his left arm.

Fortunately a bare-footed local wanders out
from the brush with his out-of-town cousin.
They belong to that 4-Runner there.

Unfortunately he looks at us suspiciously—
as one eyes wayward ones who have a problem
that one does not want to turn into one's own.
No, I don't have any way to tow you, the man shakes
his head. But we chat anyway. Maybe it's getting
around to sharing stories about flying planes,
but suddenly the stranger is more relaxed.

Fortunately he actually does have a rope.

Unfortunately it's a decades old, grizzled
neon thing off a boat, barely fit for a water skier.
Chronos ties Eagle Scout knots under our bumper
and around the 4-Runner that drags us in its wake
all seven-and-something miles up. Wholesome
umber irises keep contact with the stranger in
the mirror. Chronos steers and grins and gets
tire drift. At the top in the meadow the frays
are unknotted. I flash peace from the passenger
seat as their Toyota pulls away.

Fortunately alongside the highway it doesn't
take long to determine that if the soaked air
filter is removed then the engine runs again.
We creep back through the pooled water the
way we came—this time at a snail's pace. I prop
the filter up to dry, heater blowing on high,
while we rumble up 101 toward giant Paul
Bunyan and Babe the Blue Ox.

I AM AN
OUTSIDER

Go in Love's Corolla, south past the mushroom
shop on I-5 and turn toward the rolling hills with
registered heritage towns. Somewhere out here
there's a ranch with a white horse she learns to ride.
When we pull up the younger one is sweaty with
no shirt, swinging an ax. *I'm Running Bear* he
says with an outstretched hand. The older one's
in Wranglers and a western button-down. His
black braid runs long out the back from under
a cowboy hat. *Burton*, he says. *They call me
Chief White Buffalo Stands.*

Burton hustles Running Bear around (who
never seems to be doing it right) until he takes
the ax himself and splits the last logs. *The fire
will go for a few more hours* he says. *We have
to get these grandfathers hot.* I am an outsider
but we've been invited to sit in a lodge tonight.

When I sit in ceremony the first thing I learn
is everything has a reason—it all rests on the
particulars. Of red and yellow and white and black.
Where the bear skull is. What cardinal direction
the back door faces. How the women enter. How
the men enter. What songs the leader sings.

When the doors are closed, it's blacker than
anything. Burton throws cedar chips in the pit of
hot stones and electrifying embers crackle the
void. There are six rounds of steam. The old women
are draped in layers of dresses and shawls and one
is crumpled over, coughing in the heat. The old
men sit with robust bellies, red, stoic and refuse
water. Everyone here is cousin, brother, uncle, aunt.

Burton calls the seventh-go the cowboy round
and seems impressed we stay. Tiny sips of breath
up the nostrils. In the dark bend over close
to the ground, looking for the air that doesn't
burn. Between the prayers we offer and that last
purifying pass, the real stories escape. The scabs
come off. The wounds lay bare, rung out here. Love
sobs next to me and I can't tell where our pain
ends and these peoples' begins. All of it emerging
and merging just like the sweat and the tears.

THE VOICE SAYS GO HOME
AND I LISTEN

———

I sit at our kitchen table with a side pony like Nancy
Drew and Mama Bear's in the chair next to me with
Jimmy Hendrix stretched wide over her swelling
belly. She talks in alien coos to the toddler while
she grows another one. Those same silly sounds she
makes to scare me, hanging upside-down over the
rail from my top bunk with a flashlight on her face
when we are inseparable teens.

We wander down my mama's dusty hometown roads,
between palm trees on summer vacation. We walk
through the drive-thru at Taco Bell and lose count
of shooting stars snuggled in sleeping bags on the
trampoline. The boys always like her more. For a
long time I think I like her more than I like boys.

When I move a thousand miles away I don't say
good-bye. Every time I come back to visit and then
leave again, we don't say good-bye. I know how she
hates good-byes.

When she comes to L.A. Chronos puts her on the
back of his bike and does a hundred-mile-an-hour
wheelie through the Sepulveda tunnel. Her cheeks
are rosy when she tells me through a grin how
much fun it is. A month later after she goes home,
she calls to tell me she's gonna be a Mama Bear.

I don't know if she believes in god, but she asks me,
real serious one day, to be that baby's god mama.

When I weave between the real and the not real
and the yarn of me unravels until I'm not sure what
remains then the voice says *go home* and I listen.
I retreat here where there are baby steps and it's
easy to be one thing I am—Mama Bear's best friend.

I paint the wall gold in the bedroom that will
belong to Chronos and me. But then she decides
she and Lumberjack will keep that one. So in the
other room I paint a wall bright blue around my
big window that frames her wildwood landing.

BREATHING IN, MOUNTAIN

Keep driving up Canaan past the speeding
sweeper where god lives then onto Apiary and
there will be a sign. The gate's always open and
an old red hose truck sits under a wooden eve.
Go down a ways and the main lodge is logs,
three-sided with a sturdy rock fireplace.

They stopped cutting the trees down here
sometime in the forties. All around they keep
logging them on rotation but at Wilkerson
they make us feel small again. A meadow flows
from the lodge's open side. Everything is deserted.
We light a fire like we own this place.

I spread my red, white and navy poncho
on the dusty wooden planks.

Breathing in, mountain. Breathing out, forward fold.
Hamstrings scream as I bend myself over sturdily.
Breathing in, straight spine. Breathing out, plank.

Running Bear strolls to the other end and sits
on a picnic table. He tunes his flute while rain pelts
the metal roof, cascading from steep angles
in a ceaseless water curtain.

Notes, exquisite, evaporate and return,
dripping down my nape.

Breathing in, warrior. Breathing out, plank.
Breathing in, warrior. Breathing out, plank.

Breathing in, mountain.

"THE MOST PENETRATING PREACHERS"[†]

---

*...they struggle with all the force of their lives
for one thing only: to fulfill themselves according
to their own laws, to build up their own form,
to represent themselves...Whoever knows how
to speak to them, whoever knows how to listen
to them, can learn the truth. They do not preach
learning and precepts, they preach, undeterred
by particulars, the ancient law of life.*

—Hermann Hesse

Today I lay in the crunchy leaves of this homey
oak pulled skyward where branches sway sovereign
and Chronos' foot lofts into my world view.

I walk through an exploded alder and sit alone
in the sculpted stump throne and finger the fresh
initials of a chain-saw wielding Lumberjack and
mourn the grandeur of fifty years turned into
raw timber pyre.

We walk on the red carpet where giants
gingerly perch, shallow roots in our Mother
fueling endless triumph in a duel with gravity.
There's a creek and Chronos hears the future falling.
When a tree erupts, years later,
I am here for the sermon.

[†] With great gratitude to Hermann Hesse's
Bäume. Betrachtungen und Gedichte

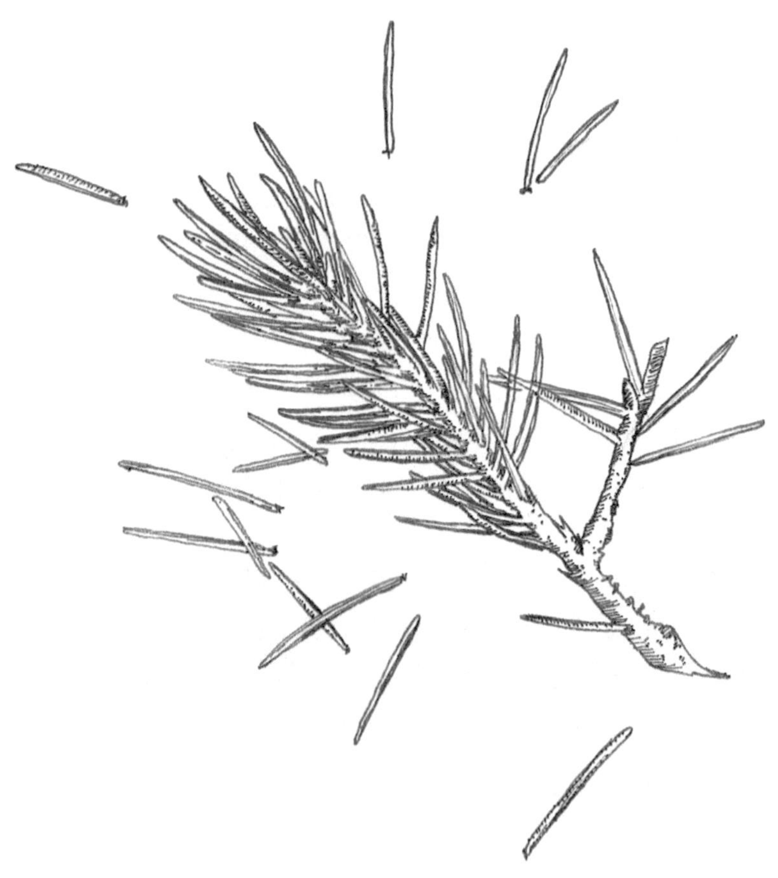

THEN
JANUARY

——

Leaves mushy and brown, frost to mud to frost.
The alders only bark, peppered all over.
Veiny and anxious, splintered branches tangle.
The fir here or there is strong and silent,
        wisely comfortable in this chill.

I go to the forest to pick a branch to fashion
            a hoop for a dream catcher.
Running Bear tells me that a green branch is the way,
        amusedly watching every twig snap,
                uninterested in becoming a circle
                        out of a straight line.

I walk past the stump throne, shrunken, slick
        and smaller than when it stands freshly slain.

I pull at a green twig hanging above and
          easily peel a length away.

It gently bows (though hardly round)
          and I am satisfied.

On the walk inside I stop still.
          Deep voices roll from shop doors.
                    The sky is whipped cream.

The branch makes a lop-sided circle, the
          old green thread breaks when
                    I'm half-through.
I watch frustration circle enjoyment. Loop,
          tighten, loop, tighten, loop, unknot, tighten.

I pluck a crystal and a stone from the hot
          pink spaceship where I keep treasures,
tie them to my web with three duck feathers
          and admire the crooked creation
                    that I will give a new friend.

"CHOP WOOD,
CARRY WATER"

Before enlightenment, chop wood, carry water.
After enlightenment, chop wood, carry water.

—Zen Proverb

I find the bike tail light swimming deep
in a corner of a tall box in the garage.
I wash the charger contacts with alcohol
so the red bulb starts to flash.
I find the loaned movie to return
in the shiny, homeless DVDs.
I wash the oatmeal dishes and
I zip my black ankle boots.

IT'S BEEN IN THE FAMILY
FOR YEARS

———

When you cook in cast iron, it gets an essence—
a knowing breath of all the meals passed through
there. There's a word for it in Cantonese; *Wok hay.*
I learn it from Anthony Bourdain.

I take my cast iron from my mama's kitchen,
buried down deep in the back of a corner cupboard.
The dust is thick and sticky with grease.

Hey what are you doing with that pan? daddy asks.
Taking it home where I'll use it I say. Well don't get
rid of that thing. It's been in the family for years.

I clean it and rub it down with oil to re-season.
While the pan gets nice and black the house
gets smoky until it burns my eyes.

Oil in the pan. Sear New York strip on both sides.
Four minutes each, let it rest for fifteen. Fry quail
eggs in the drippings, one, two, three, four,
five little gold rings. I like miniature things.

Rinse with hot water, scrub with sea salt.

Oil in the pan, perfect sweet potato cubes.
Until they're soft and ready to broil brown.

Rinse with hot water, scrub with sea salt.

Oil in the pan, chicken thighs with seasoning.
Stir fry Romanesco broccoli.

Rinse with hot water, scrub with sea salt.

Oil in the pan, duck eggs now, one side
all crispy edges to top oatmeal.

Rinse with hot water, scrub with sea salt.

WHEN MY PARENTS
ARE PEOPLE

———

Later over at Cousin Don's I stare down a
        portrait of my chipmunk-cheek, obese
                nineteen-year-old self.

I hear Dido yip in the other room.
        String-cheese to make up for
                the pup's diabetes shot.

Kuni sits noble and ninety-something
        at the kitchen counter—
                How are ya, Ash?

Dawn Marie's skirt sparkles like a mermaid fin.
        She got a new sweater at the Goodwill today.
                It has kitties she proclaims.

I got a new sweater at the Goodwill yesterday.
        It's men's size giant, imported and made of
                anti-bacterial plant-fiber I proclaim.

Later in the bar of Bing's Chinese American
        Restaurant for my parents'
                twenty-fifth anniversary,
        there's a slow-talking man who buys a round
                and hugs my daddy.

The man goes home then daddy has another one
        while he tells me about finding him first.
                It's icy the morning that man
                        is a teenager trapped
                                in a car hanging off
                                        an embankment.

Daddy breathes for him for more than twenty
        minutes en route to the trauma center.
                I was sure I'd never see him alive
                        after I found him in that car.

Sadness wells in my daddy's eyes.
He's alive but he was never quite
the same after that. And he knows it.

I excuse myself to the bathroom
where I take a selfie with a samurai.

The moon is slivers away from the
wolf of a few nights past.
The fog is heavy.
The gravel glitters.

I don't know, to this day, how we got him out.

The forest feels dead
and I crave the first day of spring.

HEALING
TAKES NUTRIENTS

——

Sleep until noon today. I shower. I make
small talk at the kitchen counter while two
pregnant ones make baby shower invites
for the one with the bigger belly. I cook peaches
that I pick from a tree and slice and freeze
for a rainy day like today. Fry them up in
bacon grease and let them simmer for ages.
I roll out gluten free pie crust with the speed
of a novice and cut it into pop-tart size pieces.
By the time I am half through the four-year-old
has sniffed the rolling pin and other exotic
kitchen tools and wants to help.

Chronos, upstairs with the swelled up knee
from surgery two days before, is appreciative
of hand-pies and eats four of them. I find them
tastier cool (which seems backwards) but still
don't consider them a great feat (as I suspect
will be the case when I eye-ball two cups of flour
up to the shortest line on the mixing bowl and
gracefully dump a glob of egg and vinegar froth
on myself and the floor and then solve the problem
by adding a whole egg and just a smidge more
vinegar). There is no room for horseplay in baking.
For superior results, precision is demanded.

I return downstairs for something or another.
I clean the baking mess. He texts emojis
from upstairs begging for more pie.

I decide it's a good idea to burn the bag
of personal papers I clean out filing (yesterday).
The four-year-old wants to play with the fire.
The little one wants the smoke out of her eyes.
Mama Bear brings more fuel for the flame.

We roast the babies' hot dogs over fast-dwindling orange leaps of bill envelopes and birthday wrap. By the time we are back inside Lumberjack is home with take-out from the place with the red sign that has their four-year-old's favorite sweet and sour chicken.

I sit on the couch while Mama Bear sneaks an episode of *Criminal Minds* and the babies are splashing in the tub upstairs. I watch a deranged man clamp a portion of his forearm with medical forceps and use a syringe to extract liquid from an alien object squiggling beneath his skin.

I am unmotivated to cook but healing takes nutrients. I quickly scrub gold potatoes and cube them skin-on and plop them in boiling water. The broccoli is stir-fried in butter. I squish out lamb burger patties and wash my hands twice then season and fry until potatoes need smashed. I take two plates upstairs and leave the kitchen to clean later.

There's too much pink salt on the lamb but not
to the point of ruin. He manages to pick through
half of dinner before his appetite fails. The food
is delicious. Pain pills make it not matter. I finish
mine and then clean the kitchen.

A mason jar of water taunts plants on the window
ledge. I pick it up to give them drinks, noting the
microscopic buds at the end of a succulent petal
I am propagating. I move it to a pot with a bit
damper soil. I feel impatient for these babies
to finish arriving.

The room is messy. There are piles of pillows
and afghans crocheted by someone else's
great-grandmother. Clothes discarded in situ,
gravitationally puddled from bodies. A couple
of plates. An empty hamper. Motorcycle armor.
Wooden crutches and a foam leg brace. The light
is warm. The earth object mobiles hang still.
The solar powered money cat. A meditating Christ.
The nude blue lady gesturally sculpted in clay. A
worn, framed poster of Klimt's lovers. They all stare.
I sit motionless in my green upholstered chair.

SACRED
SUNDAY

Aaaaa-shee. The little one calls.
Gotta say it louder, I hear Mama Bear prompt.
Aaaaaaaaaa-SHEE! she says
     with more excitement.
The older one joins in. They want to play.

I find my feet and the new natural bug spray.
Chronos wants me to spray him just because
     it smells good.

I go outdoors where one of them is crying from
injury until, sniffles under control,
     she's back in the game.

I flop with babies on the trampoline.

When bugs finally shoo us inside then
        sword fights commence—
a Disney prince's sword and its purple hull
        as an opponent.

Soon Mama Bear has a light saber and I have
a serving spoon and the twenty-month-old
is naked, wearing sparkle fairy wings while
        she yells on-guard
and does battle to protect her honor.

Sunday nights always get crazy around here
        Mama Bear says.
It always seems like it's on a Sunday.

Giggles fill the kitchen and the electric white
halogen bulb burns bright long after ten.

My god-babies' faces will look
        different again tomorrow.
The four-year-old will have learned
one more sixteen-year-old-ism.

Someday Mama Bear and I will conjure
        a wisp between, glancing to boundless
sprites who attack with plastic swords
        deep into Sunday eve.

IN THE
DIARY'S MARGIN

―

I wish the things I wrote were prettier
I wish they used fancy words
the kind of words that would
make my great aunt get
the cloth napkins out
I wish the things I wrote
were sophisticated
like that

Like the girls back when
who can do their own hair
without bumps and lumps
the ones who always pick out better
nail polish
the ones who always have better
Lip Smackers

I don't have much to write about
that strays far from these truths of mine
I'm just not sure
what the hell is going on here
have you figured it out?

I stop writing to
go check the chicken
stock downstairs.
I am anxious suddenly
that it might be boiling
over and making me look
like an idiot.
Lumberjack is in
the kitchen we share
turning his first kill
of the season into
some kind of
spicy meat thing.

I tell him about
the Northern Lights.
How they might show
after midnight.
Or maybe tomorrow.
He seems surprised.
I hope we can see them.

Cloth napkins or not
it's a pretty thing
this novelty of planet Earth

We save pop cans for milk
instead of five dollar words
where I come from

but I'll be damned
I understand why
one could use some
to
explain
all of
this

THERE SHIVERS A
LITTLE THING AT THE SPINE

———

From one tip to the other.
Pooling into orbs that quake your belly. Your hips
rock. Your shoulders shake.
Your crumpled serpent raises its head. Arches up.
Chin tosses back.
The light explodes from your chest and this place is
broken.
      And now

      somewhere

      else

      entirely

      the sun shines of you.

I pick up the sand in my hands.

It runs
      through my fingers
            and is carried to the sound
                  of the immeasurable sea
                        which is calling me
                        home.

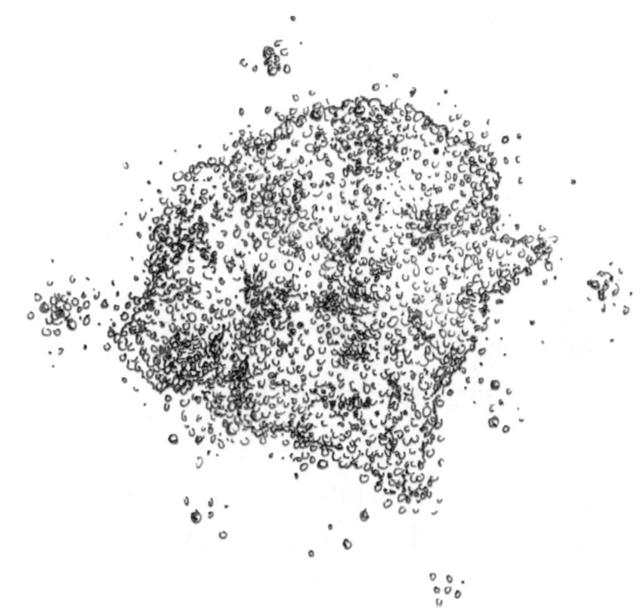

THE STORY THAT GETS TOLD BEFORE BERRY PICKING

Well if you're going to pick berries, Gramp adds,
make sure you pick a gallon coffee can clear full
and then leave it out for the steers.

Now, father! Gran exclaims. You see, years ago
I was out picking and left a full can tucked in
the bushes. When I came back to get it, it was
empty and there was that white steer of ours,
face pinker than pink with berry juice.

The steers come up curious. Scan, pluck, drop.
Repeat. My left hand is sweaty in my leather
moto glove. My right hand is covered in juice and
sticker kisses. Minuscule brown spines crumble
from the berries. It's hot. Mama's iced tea is good.

Dawn Marie wants to go inside just a handful into
the heat. Mama lasts a bit longer but says faintly
I need to head back up to cool.

There's a lot dead now, dried on the vine, and
scanning becomes more numbing. The creek is low
this time of year, a new barbed-wire fence runs on
the property's side and I miss the wide open place
I remember from being small.

I gather the berry crates and walk up the hill.
Hey, sissy? Gramp calls from the porch. *Come in
for a minute. We have something for ya.* I walk
toward the concrete steps topped with the torn
screen. *Aunt Deb left this for you for your birthday.*
He hands me a long mirror, flimsy and black
trimmed, made for hanging on doors.

SMOOTH THE
MARIONBERRY JAM

———

The rooster is learning to crow.
    The ducks smarm and the rays are warm
        on this tattered spread.

I turn toward Chronos and he pulls his arm
    underneath—in minutes we fast-forward
        to asana three. The little
            bigger spoon. The bigger
              little spoon.

Shuffles and screeches in the downstairs—
    the rise of morning play.
        He groans and turns over.
          His ass is perfect
              when he leaves to pee.

While he's gone I lay and naked text
        about laying and naked texting until
            I get out of bed and
                put on a wizard robe.

I take a selfie in the mirror
        to prove I have a wizard robe.
            I wear this gown to brown enough
                tater tots and scramble enough
                    eggs for four people
                        even though there
                            are two.

I toast the nut bread,
        smooth the marionberry jam
            and sprinkle the Himalayan salt
                pinch by pinch over it all.

I drink the rest of the orange juice from the carton.
        The coffee is heavy on cream.
            The phone rings.

THINGS WE CAN REMEMBER

There's the stately, high-back (but worn)
club chair, a European-looking cream
recliner with footstool near it, a matching
leather loveseat facing the flat screen TV
and one black metal folding chair where
Kuni sits, a walker right in front of her.
A single striking dahlia in a crystal
vase on the sill.

My mind is incapable of plucking apart
her spick-and-span abode for the sake
of furnishing this room here.

Her back is hurting her today.
There's apparently nothing more to do.
I wonder how much trouble I'd get in
for slipping her a Cheeba Chew.

Why do you sit on the floor, Ash?
with a motion to the empty seats.
I like to, I say. *Well. All right.*

The TV isn't on. She must have just returned
from dinner. I'm grateful there's no evening
news, Jeopardy or Wheel of Fortune. *There's
probably a baseball game on.* I don't mind
baseball but she never reaches for the remote.

She wants to go home but can't live alone.
When she reminds herself out loud of the
address where she's lived for over two decades,
she adds *I'd like to get back out there.* I know
that somehow her vision of home isn't the (now
dis-arranged) single-level ranch streets away,
but instead the old white farmhouse her
and Cleaver live in out on Berg Road.
Before they move into town. Before he falls
and is paralyzed on my seventh birthday.
Before he dies on my seventeenth birthday.

Before the years I spend sitting at her grand
wood table with cloth napkins in front of the
gilded mirror under the dining room skylight.
Her brain remembers a different home. Even
if she goes home, it still won't feel like home.

I charm her with young person stories
about riding motor bikes and I explain what
kombucha is. She's confused about how
someone left the weekly menu on her couch.
*I have a key, you see. How did someone else
get in here?* I don't have the heart to tell her
everyone on staff probably has a key.
She fingers her Black Hills gold bracelet
subconsciously.

*How do you think they wash
these windows?* she asks.

*There's probably a company who
comes to wash them each season.*

*Well good. I don't mind washing the
insides, but I'm not washing the outsides.*

We are three stories up.

*I don't think they want you to.
No step ladders for you, remember?*

She gets a guilty look on her face.

*Yeah. I'm not supposed to do that.
I learned my lesson.*

I wonder if lessons are much good to learn
if you can't remember.

I spend too much time hiding under
the brim of my hat. The long silences
don't quite cross the threshold into
awkward. But it's fucking awkward
when dying hangs in the air.

I long to be able to tell her
everything I see—

that there's nothing to be scared of.
That we've both done it over and
over before.

But it's all I can do to remember.

I WATCH
THE SMOKE CURL

Hard then soft then back arc,
    leg strain and all the warmth
        is slick and smears.
I get a towel with my clean hand and
    wash my hands in pitch-dark
        with Geranium soap then
            snuggle up close, petting gently
until his purs are rhythmic and even.

    I should light the sage.
        I should smoke some flower.
        I should.

I slip off the bed and kneel at the altar.
    I watch the smoke curl.

A box of photos

                    under Babe's jewelry box.

A small square, standing legs bare
      wrapped in an afghan in the courtyard of
         our Los Angeles lair, ratty moccasins
         and bed hair bookending
            my sleepy smile.

We look like babies—five years takes a toll.

A close-up of the side of the painted lover's face, golden
      with beach, cheek full of stubble.

The black and white strip where
      I'm the prettiest I'll ever be,
                fresh in love
      with silly hats.

Salty drops on these sense windows.
      I hate the wrinkle between my brows.
      I catch my ghost in the
         mirror on the door.

I look at this big life,

                                  so infinitesimal.
              All of these things I keep as me.
                  It's quiet.

                    I can't take any of it with me.

I take another toke and blow my nose.
          I get close to the one in the bed.
                I settle for rubbing my hands over
                        flesh that won't be here forever.

                        so I have it now.

SOME AREN'T EVEN MIRRORS AT ALL

I am the Smokey Mirror, because I am looking at myself in all of you, but we don't recognize each other because of the smoke in-between us. That smoke is the Dream, and the mirror is you, the dreamer.

—Don Miguel Ruiz

When I see the opposite of my reflection
      —how I really am—it bothers me a little.
That right is left and left is right and it all
      just seems a bit backwards.
I'm not used to seeing it like it is.

Walking down the breezeway carrying books.
      If only I had thighs like that.
         But not those arms.
            Do I look thinner than
               when I checked last?

There's the skinny-black-framed-one hanging
        with 3M tape on the back of my bedroom door.

The tiles in the only bathroom at my parents' start
        high up the wall. First they only see
                the top of my head.

The gilded frame gold under the skylight
        behind Kuni's dining table.

The giant one hanging with screws and plastic tabs
        over the daveneau at Gran and Gramp's.

The rectangular ones in the worn,
        yellow-tile bathrooms at school.

The one in a dressing room that hawks
        illusions of tall and thin.

The one in the bedroom on Sundale. (Where
        the photographs of wordly destinations
                hang—labeled by my hand—and faux-
                        French-styled miniature trunks
                stack neatly at the end of
                        our heavily linened bed.)

A friend walks out of my condo bathroom one day
and says *I look hot in your bathroom.*
Really, *that is one flattering mirror.*

When I go to leave the house I double back to the
full length closet doors for one last check
even though I already have my shoes on.

All these mirrors.

One sees me expand.
One sees me shrink.
One pleasantly surprises.
One begs me to pick at my face
until red welts grow.

Some aren't even mirrors at all;
just clean windows
where I can get a fix between.

AUGUST
TWELFTH

It rains through the night. The kind
that raps through my sleep and enters
my dreams and makes me know that
there's water falling even while the
improbable and absurd roam my mind.

I turn off the alarm and get up forty
minutes later. Into the shower with
Chronos where I shave my legs with
a dull razor and wonder if it's been long
enough in between apricot scrub washes
to keep my sensitive face from breaking
out again. I rub on lotion and lavender
oil and lament the dirty clothes hamper—
full of everything I want to wear. I dig
through the weekend road trip duffel
to find clean panties and faded Levi's
and pull a purple silk shirt from my closet.

I drive so he can smoke. I'm stuck behind
a white work truck. Then a big rig hauling
strong, noble logs. And the curves and dips
of the long mountain road take longer than
they should. I turn down the side street to get
on the highway, out-pacing the semi waiting
for too much traffic to pass, and fly by the
run-down house with the garden exploding
in every color of summer flower.

Fifty miles later I round up the presents
I need to mail. And get a cold brew with
a zest of orange. I watch the half and half
cloud the cup. I kiss Chronos goodbye
and I take off again. From the freeway out
to the country there's eighteen miles of
suburban sprawl and traffic lights
followed by ten miles of sweepers sunk
into farmland. The tape deck broke
yesterday. I sing through the lights, off key
but committed, my favorite Christian hymn
from childhood. I follow the Schwann's
man through the fields and corners.
I watch the gas gauge drop.

THERE'S A LITTLE MORE MAGIC
IN THE VERISIMILITUDE

Sometime soon desires are satiated and bellies
are not and it's into a summer storm for sustenance.
The car ride is quiet and brimming
with the nagging insecurities mind likes to
cultivate after I expose myself the first time,
naked and trembling. *Those may be bullshit.*

I love my roast beef sandwich. And the baked brie.
I love the grey in this unfamiliar beard. I try to
love the flamboyant try-hard sitting two tables over.
But I'm not quite that good at loving.

There's no gluten free peanut butter cookies,
but disappointment is welcome.
Real life has disappointments.

The rain has stopped and the shifts are hard
on the drive back. There's a little less magic in
the mystery. There's a little more magic in the
verisimilitude. I use the bathroom and wash
my hands with the soap his hands smell of
and I wonder what scent it is.

Thunderstorms leave the sky humming.
I keep the window down. The air conditioner
blows hot. The traffic crawls. My brain stays
still. Airy and open—free.

THE FUTURE
IS ENTIRELY FOREIGN

—

I sit on a beach in Ventura
      when I see
            time   splinter.

My motorcycle jacket under my rear.
A wall of water rolling, a dome of air,
      a full circle horizon.

Everything unfolds from nothing and somehow,
in these same atoms, I see one future and end up
      in a different one.

Branches of possibility jutting out from here
and splitting again and once I go
      left, right, left, right, right,
the future is entirely foreign
      to left, left, right, left, right.

So now I know there's a future me over there,
        and not just that one.
Infinite past and future me's
        being all the things I don't choose,
look over, am a little late for.

I saw you two in a dream before we met each other
Aristotle says. You know, like how sometimes I see
things? I see things and then when they happen,
sometimes I just go along with it (just like the dream
it happens) and sometimes I make it end differently.

After I see the time split I start to wonder:
        Well then, is there a way to get over there?
I start to see that the windows are small
and unassuming where I can leap to other tracks.

Leaving the house a minute later.
   Choosing the red cup.
      Smiling when I look up.

I saw this before in a dream Aristotle says.
   Well, what happens then? I ask.
He smiles, silent until:
   I can't figure out a way to tell you without
making it end like the dream.

THEY CALL IT THE NECTAR OF THE GODS

Nestled in on the Neskowin coast,
I've been here for eighteen hours
    staying at Jesus's cousin's friend's family's
      vacation cottage.

There's an old swing outback
made from a car bench seat.
    I curl up on it and watch the grasses sway
      until he comes to sit next to me.

His eyes I'm looking at are new
from three weeks ago, but I'm sure
      I know Jesus since some other life.

Here in this one we walk down the
beach to Proposal Rock sharing irises of sapphire
      sky and hints of wave water sparkle.

When we leave it's nearly sun down.
I smoke a bowl   sticky with resin.

He drives an Alero, white and long.
We crawl through sleepy streets,
      maybe in circles.

In a yard babies shout
while a sprinkler glints in the golden sun
      soup—we all simmer.

Water drops fall on our
windshield and time swells
      for just that block.

From the front seat of his Olds I watch
the place behind my eyes get juicy
            and a gush of ecstasy trickles
                down my throat.

        They call it the nectar of the gods
he says, his lightning bolts
            brushing my thigh.

        I'm quiet with Jesus
(and these babies I never know).
        Enshrined in millenia-long sun-showers,
                I open my eye.

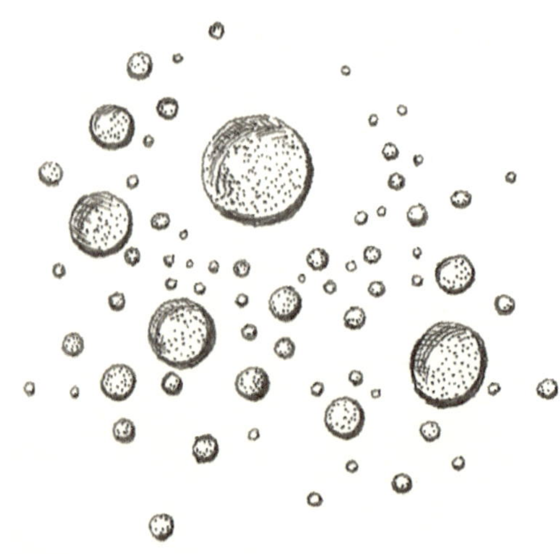

I ARC ALONG
THIS FUSE

———

It has been shown, the fingers tremble,
and the body quivers at times...

—Indian Shaker Church, December 17, 1910

The rope that runs up and down is the rope
to the gods made from the ancestors, Jesus offers
off-hand as we lay on wool blankets in a dimly lit
studio, spent from shaking. *The rope that runs*
perpendicular to that is the rope between
masculine and feminine.

The rope that goes

> *down,*
> *down,*
> *down...* he says.

                                        up.

                               up,
And the other that stretches   *up,*

There's a tug at my coccyx.
My hips drop toward my knees and tilt slightly,
fully straightening the last few vertebra.
A flutter continues there and a beat begins
barely higher, floating deep in the center of my
hip bones. I bounce into the sinking posture,
weighty with bent knee. Density waves from

left

                        to

                                            right.

A white light rope anchors me
through the floor.
Through the foundation.
Through the earth.
Out the other side and past all the stars.
Just pointing down.
The down-est down.
The empirical

down.

The rocking motion shifts front to back. The
energy flows upward, through my belly and
into my chest. He leans into me. I come into a
shallow backbend

     with
          no
               fear
                    of
                         falling,
                         adjusting
                  for
               every
        shift,
               anticipated
                     or
                            not.

As long as I trust it, as long as I don't think too
hard. As long as I don't stop to think at all.
I simply get pulled into the gravity
of this holy energizing force.
He clucks and clicks as it
hovers around

                        of its own accord.

                        up...
                up,
        up,
And

I feel a tug
at my crown.
I am pulled
a few inches
higher out of
this settled
spiritual sag,
suddenly
tensioned by
the sizzling
cord that
stretches up   up.
through the
ceiling, through
the first and
second floors,
out of this house,
through any
see-able skies,
beyond all the stars,
forever, just exactly

The softness of that neck pressed against the side
of my face. His sandy strands tangled in mine—
stuck against lips, wispy around shoulders.

I arc along this fuse,
stuttered for knowing
while there's no one here to know anything.
Sense-making suspended.
Ultimate knowing gifted.
A direct download of this sacred alignment.

There's literally an internal compass.

I live here as long as I can before giggling.

Tongues flutter faint as my body involuntarily
strains when forces turn against a constricted
Vishuddha. I feel a jolt emanate from his palm
that burrows between my shoulder blades, drills
into the center of my chest spinning upward,
quickly snaps my head back and settles deep into
my brain stem. Then I feel the same pulse fall

     downward,
     exploding   out   of   my   heart-chest.

When the resistance softens then a throaty
rumble rushes from a roll of my belly.

His *tskkk* transforms to a satisfied *ahhh*.
He gently scoops hair off my neck and his lips
inhale sharply against the nape and I feel clarity.

Then he's lying flat and I'm pressed exactly against
him and the vibration intensifies, piercing from
crown to heel and simultaneously, perpendicularly
through the chest.

Our
bodies
short-circuit life-force
in
every
direction.

My pineal gland melts. I shudder and quake, fully
clothed, writhing here. I laugh at this absurdity.

The cross actually means something.

I watch the horrific torture tool of my childhood
religion transform into a grand spectacle of
boundless energy pulled along these two axes
that guide all things.

It feels so good, he says.
You're fucking silly, I say.

Not having many words to say about
all this magic
        that's real.

THESE THINGS WILL NEVER HAPPEN
QUITE LIKE THAT AGAIN

———

Jesus will never sit at that table with three sides

(spilling with fresh juice
and fragrant mint
and goat cheese feta
and half-sipped orange peel tea
and steaming lentil lamb stew
and spoonfuls of tzatziki
and shards of dark chocolate)

just that particular way again.

I remember that while it is happening and so
I watch real close.
And it is beautiful.

All these things that can never happen again.

When I go to the bathroom
                                            (the second time)

the wrapper for his chamomile shampoo
sits just so next to the fingernail clippers
and every speck of dust clings noble in its
independence
on the wide window sill. The light is blue.

When our skin touches, softness explosion.

When I'm consumed with those eyes—
        of a wolf,
                of a lion,
                        of my Mother the Earth,
                        of my lover.

When the doings and undoings of a whole other
dimension   wind up there

in that darkness behind our ears.

These things will never happen quite like that again.
I remember that while it is happening.
And it is beautiful.

That's really all there is to do now, all of the time.
Remember
                                    this
will never happen again.

                    And it's goddamn beautiful.

SOME DAYS
THE SONGS COME

My life is full of tulips lately.

And mowing grass.

I haven't been toking much;
ropes tugging stronger than ever.

Yoga.
Dishes.
Make the bed.
Wear summer clothes on the hot spring days.

You've visited my dreams a time or two.
So many dreams lately—alien worlds
and foreign times.

Some days the songs come. I like those days
especially.
			But really I like all of the days.

I'm making another rattle
(found a perfect gourd at the Goodwill).

Straw bale gardening in the backyard;
starts almost ready to plant.

I hope you're in love even as I'm comforted
that I know it's where you live.
I see my reflection in your light.
Namaste, lover.
Ah sha ta ti ti num ohm.

TO ATTEMPT SUCH THINGS ON ONE'S OWN (THE FIRST TIME)

While I'm walking past the small, well-lit alley
      I am thinking about birds.
The freedom of flight.
The branches to light upon.
The beautiful simplicity of stacking twigs
      to make a home.
Plentiful bugs to eat.
Feathers to pride and preen.
Precious eggs that I know not what
      will manifest from but that I guard
      with my life.
I am thinking about being a bird.
It's no small feat to turn into a bird.
I did it twice.
But under the supremely careful supervision
      of that shaman lover.

To attempt such things on one's own (the first time)
        would be ill advised.
It's a task supreme to find your way back.
You've got to have someone around trustworthy
        to help with that.
If I let go and float into that fuzzy orb there?
If I let go and sink into this endless well here?
If I let go
        will I find my way back?
Will I even want to
        after what I find there?
Will I even remember
        that I want one of these body-things?
Or will I forget
        for awhile
        and then again
        become all-consumed with desire
        for skin?
Orbs of gods, wells of ancestors
        keep coming back for skin.
I keep coming back
        to touch yours.

THIS SMOKING PATIO I'M ON

The red door I'm looking for is only one
　　　street more.
Around the jutting archipelago of trashcans,
　　　in the smoking patio, fenced on the
　　　sidewalk, is Sierra.

It's the night I meet her sister, Marla.
Sharp wit, sharper eyes, octopus necklace.
Sierra says it's all the molly and the
　　　orgasms that have her so relaxed at
　　　the end of visiting you.

I chuckle uncomfortably.

Sit shyly, left to reconcile this socially inept
    pretty girl I apparently am sitting here.
I pull at my skirt when I walk even though
    it's plenty long.
I sip sparkles while they go pick their songs.

This smoking patio I'm on opens to a bar that's
    tiki-themed.
It's empty still but soon the karaoke lounge
    will be filled on a Tuesday night
    with all the ones here to sing
    love songs to Sierra.

I only go to bars for Sierra, Marla says.
Me, too.

SOMEONE ELSE'S CIGARETTE SMOKE

My boxy blazer in seventies wool
    smells like someone else's cigarette smoke.
The sleek gold leaf that sits on the lapel
    is one of the brooches in those costume
    jewelry boxes I get when Babe dies.

I remember going over to help.
To *Violet's Villa*—her skinny single-wide
    sitting in the mobile home park.
Aunt Babe hides Fostoria crystal in the cupboards
    and watches the Home Shopping Network.
The wood paneled walls are sticky with
    three decades of nicotine.

The albums show Babe and Bernice (her
        sidekick sister) regal in polyester suits.
Once, when Babe gets in a tiff with
        Gran (back when they both wear
        horn-rimmed glasses) Babe hangs up on her.
Gran and Babe don't speak for years.

Babe's memory is going as she sits legs crossed
        in a seafoam sweatsuit and wears all of her
        diamond rings and pushes long manicured
        nails into the buttons of the remote.

Babe goes every week for a permanent and dons
        a bonnet from the door of the salon.
She smokes more than she eats.
Mama tries to get her to drink Ensure.

The soapy sponge sticks in the smoke gum,
        balling off in chunks as I drag it across the wall.

PLOT TO FIND
MERMAIDS

There's a modest white wall in this single room
that's mine for now where all the art I own
is displayed gallery style. *Do you want to see my art?*
I ask her shyly.

There's that famed poster of lip-locked lovers,
printed in the seventies with golden ink,
long since missing the cracked glass I pull off it
when I buy it from a yard sale in Inglewood.

There's the small canvas, hand painted,
of a lover by my other lover's almost-lover.
The two don't know each other when she is
an art student at Otis and he is a nude figure
model. But later she lives in the condo upstairs
and says off-hand *I'm pretty sure I painted
a picture of your friend* one day.

There's a white-on-white needle point
of Yggdrasil nestled in a matte in a frame.
I like the rumor that the tree of life
is an ash tree.

But the *pièce de résistance*, the thing
she really needs to see, is a small eight by eight
square, Kodachrome, I buy on a Saturday.
I ask the man where to find this pristine lagoon.

Detroit Lake I tell her then.
There's a mermaid cave at Detroit Lake
that we must see.

But this summer it's dry docked and the fish
are shriveled.

We find water here on this turn of
sandy shore in the Puget Sound.
I see mushroom graffiti on a troll bridge.
She hugs a tree.

I dangle Converse in my hand while we wander into
shallow sea. Way out until the ocean is lapping
at our knees. Lost in the looking out.

Giving up on the holding on.
Submerged in this.
Only being.

I turn and look down through cloudy blue
and see swirls of ghostly white.
I'm drawn closer but right before it's too close
That's a jelly!
Sierra exclaims.
Shit. It is.
Hundreds.
Everywhere.

The boldness with which we emerge
is tempered by the care of our return.

Slow to pick our way back, inch by inch
through ornate tentacles and bulbous goo.

We arrive unstung, minding the jelly,
saving our plot to find mermaids for
when there's water for Detroit Lake.

THE CATHEDRALS WE MAKE

The house has to be clean. The pillows straight. The floor swept. The carpet vacuumed. The counters sprayed and scrubbed. The bathroom tidied. The emails returned. The to-do lists downloaded from minds for attending to some other time. The bed made. Just so. Just as it should be. The plants watered, not thirsty. A watermelon chilling in the icebox. A fresh rose cut from outside. An offering to the mycelium-god. Incense heavy. The sink empty. The water pitcher full. The candles arranged. The sage burning. The lights comfortable. The earth objects hanging reverently. The air quiet. The pencils sharp and the hearts open. The water pipe clean. The joint rolled. Only then can we sit in a circle.

A tray at the center with three flickering saint
candles—Saint Jude, the Sacred Heart of Jesus,
Guardian Angel—beside a tall vase of water
(Our Lady of Guadalupe up there on the mantel).
The shell sits iridescent, the palo santo curls
smoke scent memories. Four pencils scratch
against fiber, intentions penned for the listening,
in surrendered jest to the silliness of ever being able
to know exactly how to ask for just what we need.
In all beings highest good, we ask these things.

*We did a water offering last time
so we don't have to smell like campfire.*

Plus, it's raining.

That seems all right to me.

Would you like some?

What is it?

Rose oil.

Fragrant and sweet at the sternum for me. That one dabs it close to his thyroid. The other one to each side behind the ear. Again at the heart-space for the last one, blessed and ready for orbit. Mine is ground fine in a speckled clay cup with red flowers painted on the side. A chunk of raw chocolate and steaming water, stirred to a few gulps of enchanted paste. His is piled soft like twigs in a bowl, a broken square of mayan spiced cacao resting on top. The other two have fuller mugs, more water, more chocolate, more magic. It's all ready.

The first gulp makes me gag.
The second not as much.

Can you please pass the pitcher?

Fuck, we just did that.

Here goes again.

We roll up our intentions and submerge them.
And we wait.

Comfier clothes. Lights down lower. *Damn
it's working fast.* He is lying flat on the ground.
He is sitting in a chair. He kneels over there.
I have my favorite afghan around me, sitting
hooded like a curandera, a floating impostor
with no ancestral roots that reach this life.
It begins to move, this place, separating from
the outside air right behind the window pane.
It begins to move this place. I shake and mutter
and sit ramrod straight and then slouch over
still as they burrow all through. Sweeping
the atoms into proper vibration, cleaning up
the messes I've made here in matter. Reveling
in revelation. Pummeling into knowing that
cannot be known.

My skin crawls with the same undulation that
moves the carpet and the hair that hangs in my
eyes. I can't escape places only seen before I know
language—these places I live in for so long, these
places where there can't be I. These places gated
with the demand of surrender. When the rope
uncoils and can go up, up, up and down, down,
down, that's when my hands shiver like humming
birds and my voice titters tonal and the energy
quakes palpably for the other three to hear.

I look up at Jesus, the wise, warm sage, still
sitting folded in the chair. His rope tugs,
chugging, eyes closed, forehead wide, settled
softly in the real holy glow—just like the one
of the painted saints on those dollar store
candles. The triangles jut in every direction.
The pixels get more blurry, rearranging his face
to some savior here with the un-secrets that bless
everything. When his eyes open our meditations
meet out there, where in there and out there has
no different coordinate. Here in empty space
forces of Being collide. There we move matter.

Behind me still laying still on the floor is Chronos.
His exquisite meditation blooms an architectural
dome around him—perfectly quiet, perfectly
peaceful, impeccably surrendered in perpetuity.
He lays there in that impenetrable, cool,
rejuvenating vault of knowing, resting for the time
being, making ready for the ways we shall move
careful and deliberate into lifetimes unforetold.
Patiently in tune with how things have always
been and shall always be.

The last one kneels to my right, elbow on knee,
head propped on hand. The thinker, the knower,
a cosmic Aristotle of centuries future traveled
back here on himself crouched in this living room.
Around his head like an astronaut's bubble orbits
the splendidly beautiful math-code of everything.
This last one is wide-eyed, long-lashed when he
asks *How far have we traveled this time?*

Past time, we know together. But we don't have to
say it because there where we can move matter,
in the middle, the thought-arrangements don't
need sound. There where we can move matter
in the middle, Aristotle and I know at the same
time, intimately, this stunning immortal verity of
quantum entanglement. We can tell the truth in the
smallest fraction of eternity, but only with our eyes.

I glance around in wonder at this cathedral—
high on ourselves, timeless, formless, simple,
exactly rendered as the only things we can be.
How many times have we done this? Aristotle asks.
I glance around in wonder at how many times
I've been here, just like this. Just perfectly this.

I glance around in wonder, knowing this is where
it all comes from. Over and over we come from
here to move the matter. Over and over we spring
from this perfect nothing we never quite leave,
into everything, and back dissolved again. Over
and over in every way. Oh how long we have been
here in this perfection.

I can spin atoms with my hands
and send love like cyclones
whistling through the Odin-blessed halls
of these four open-full hearts.

Tomorrow that time-traveling Aristotle says,
He's like the sage and he's like
the still-knowing-dome—

Jesus and Father Time, I say.

And you? He tells me, You're like the
Platonic ideal of love.

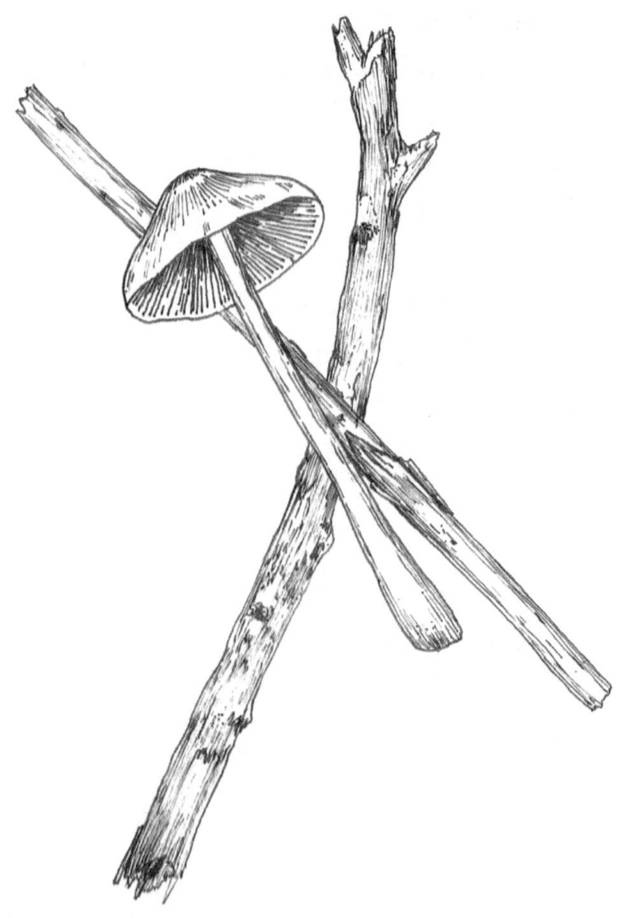

FALLING

I'm headed northbound. Road spray.
Everything's grey. Hydroplane. White knuckles.
Take a deep breath. And another one.
The freeway crosses the Columbia, birthed
wide and splayed in the valley below Wy'east.
Government Island in the middle—the place
hobos trek with make-shift packs, squeeze
through freeway walls and camp for a while.
Past Vancouver into slow moving logging towns.
Kalama, straight across the river from my
homeland. Longview, low on stench today.
Trees get taller, mist gets heavier. Traffic slows
from its hurried clip. Eighty, seventy, sixty, fifty-five.
Forty miles an hour while the water is relentless.

Holy shit.

A tidal wave washes over the center divider.
Grooved pavement pulls the old car skittish to
each side. I linger on how terrible it would be
to change a tire then chide myself for letting
such thoughts so close to manifestation.

Coming up on Olympia for that first stop.
Everything is swampy with the defroster
running warm. Brake lights are heavy
on the capital's streets. I snake through town
to the hip Mexican eatery where I hug a sibling
I never had until the month before. He's tall
and his dark hair is cropped short. There's
not much about our appearances that give it
away but I see myself in his quiet sharpness
and the way both brows crease.

It's short, the time we have here. There are
long silent pauses that leave the awkward
potential of more deeply knowing each other
for another occasion. I stop at Walgreens on
my way out of town for a birthday card, a pack
of gold foiled postcards and an iridescent
string of hanging beads for my glasses.

I wear a cape I sew myself, shrouded in asphalt
grey, a hood lined with antique green. My stockings
are sheer black with a grid of small dots, cut-off
shorts hiked into the crease of my thigh, and a shirt
silkspun golden rod, billowy at the long sleeve.
My boots clip on wet sidewalk.

I navigate the long wagon around the depths of
a parking lot lake and find myself on the freeway.
It's not twenty miles before I realize I forgot gas.
The car behind me is full of teenagers putting
in five. I fill my tank remembering scrounging for
quarters between seats, raking crumb covered
carpets to put in eighty seven cents to get to
school and home and back again.

I PAINT
A THIRD EYE

I color my face and she teases her hair,
folding it expertly over the extensions
promising pretty princess transformation.
Sierra stands in the tiny alcove bathroom
while I sit on the floor just outside the door,
scooted up to the mirror with a tub of makeup
(gone unused so long) in front of me. I paint
a third eye in the middle of my forehead
while she pens on perfect brows. I swirl the
pearlescent rainbow, rinse the brush, go again.
Three dots across high cheek bones.

Do you know how to French Braid?

*It's been so long since I got ready with
another grown lady around.*

Thanks for playing dress up with me.

Selfies before we leave.

She makes her costume too—a perfectly tufted
yellow satin mini with felted tacos at the
neckline. Her tights are nude. Fluffy white,
deftly crafted-from-trash-bag sleeves are her
only defense against the chilly autumn breeze.
I'm an oracle and I lower a bent spoon over my head.
Taco Belle grabs her Fire Sauce clutch. We both
wear cowboy boots and set out for the wild west.

Do you know what your spirit animal is?
I haven't thought about that in a while. Turtles
used to be my totem and on a vision quest once
a tiny, perfect elephant sat in an armchair beside
me across from a blazing fire. But those aren't right
anymore. *Birds*, I say. *It feels like it might be a bird
now.* All summer I see hawks and eagles soar. Over
trees. Over water. Circling as I gaze through the glass
on long yellow-line drives. One afternoon in a canoe
on Trillium Lake I watch a Bald Eagle and a hawk
dive and dart, fighting for this salamander filled
territory I float over. The eagle wins.

She talks about her affinity for foxes. Adaptable.
Swift and sharp. Cozy in a den. I chuckle at our
millennial banter—perfectly meta, selfies on
selfies, content to endlessly explore these densely
complicated human-things our soul is stuffed in
here. Might as well be fascinated while we have
to watch ourselves unfold. *It's the best show we got.*

We tuck into the pho place that feels like
Los AngelTokyo here on the streets of Sea Town.
Bump in to Unicorn Bar to use the bathroom.
More selfies in the mirror. A photo booth performance.
Paul Bunyan on the stairway. Capes, crowns and
furries. In and out quick and back on the street.

Cross walk. Wet pavement. There's the club. The
line is short now, the cover is free if you give up
your email. Dance floor sparse. More photo booth.
Stringy cobwebs. Tequila shots. Another one.
Or three. Before becoming dancing queens.
Slip through the crowd. Bathroom lines. Assess
the wilting in the mirror. Circle, circle, circle.
Stand over there.

An anonymous man with a unicorn head.
Carmen San Diego is here with Waldo.
Pikachu stops to say hi—she brings her boyfriend,
Gotta Ketchum All. The milkman is hunky. His
bearded lady sits sturdy under Abe Lincoln's hat.
Bender is there, robotic and blocky in tinfoil.

Are you All Dogs Go to Heaven?

How long did it take to paint that eye?

Taco Belle!!!!!! That's. Fucking. Brilliant.

The bar tender is a tall and lanky Elvira. Ciders, beers,
mixed drinks from the well. Grab the plastic. *Open
or closed?* Fistfuls of bills. Ping pong from that side
to the other. Pikachu is back for another round.

Damn that's a fine leotard and side pony.
Richard Simmons would be proud.

I'm a responsible mom.

Ariana Grande.

It's real hot in there. Dance floor pulsing now.
The bar tender is out of limes. Marla's here.
We find her emerging from her chariot with
pointed elfish ears. The line wraps around the
building. The rain is just starting to fall. The stand on
the corner forks over dogs covered in everything.
Netflix and Chill walks by. Another anonymous
one—sculpted-Ken-Doll-flesh and a white fox mask.
The guy behind us in line is fuzzy head to foot in a
shark suit with a shark pack on his right shoulder.

I'm Left Shark.

It turns out oracles don't actually know everything
so I tell him I'm Googling it. At the Super Bowl,
Katy Perry got freaky with the dancer to her left,
dressed like a shark. So *that's why there are sharks
everywhere tonight.* He shares his vape.
We spar verbally with line cutters until we're
under the overhang. The drops fall harder.
Finally back in. *You can dance if you wanna.*

Tequila shots? Pineapple juice chasers.
Dripping sweat. Push through, brush against,
swirl, light flash, beat drop, pulse, pulse, pulse.
Fight the current or surrender to the wave.
Back up and away, toward the wall, grind,
bump, hands everywhere.

You're just too pretty, aren't you?

I don't think that's a real thing.
(You can't be too pretty.)

You're not from here are you?
His breath smells like vomit. I shake my head.
Close eyes, feel vibes, be this pulsing thing.

I've got to go find my friend.

I'm going to get another drink.

Daylight savings. Back to two again.
We're time travelers mother fucker.
Break for a cigarette, deep breath outside.
This one's face is pretty and he's wearing Jordans.
Just got off work he says and offers me a smoke.

Can I just have a puff of yours?

What are you anyway?

What do you think I am?

We make small talk into
lighting the next one until eventually
he proposes
You just might know everything.

THIS THING
THAT HAS A NAME

A bowl of fetishes calls to be sifted. Itty bitty
bronzed pieces
of Buddha in sitting meditation. Buddha in prayer.
Jesus. Ganesha.
One I don't know. A flying mermaid?

A scaled tail curved around back. Wings
stretched wide like a totem pole.
Who is this? What is she? Why is she in me?
How do I know
she is in me when I've never seen her before?

Do you know who this is?

The lady behind the counter with the progressive
tattoos and the blunt
dark bangs answers quickly and turns to fetch
a small book
from the shelf behind her.

Naga Kanya.

She reads the passage. *Strong magical powers,
vast knowledge, bringer
of rain.*

I'm seized by this writhing winged serpent that
possesses me,
starting just weeks before.

I silently offer welcome to
this thing that has a name.

UNSPIRALING
AND BACK IN AGAIN

—

The wind whips loud and we watch the whole sound.
A saint coming through those clouds soon.
Boats on the water. High
rises, speckled window lights.
That Needle there in the middle.

The birds arrive then, unraveling fractal flight
patterns against oscillating sky—tight as a cluster,
unspiraling and back in again.

A Chorus Line Hypothesis right there in the air.
The winged beasts dart and turn and delight.
Synchronized.
One.

Watch still until the howls of laughter at this
        utter perfection are torn from our bellies.

Big, thundering guffaws pulled from the center of
                            our wombs,
        announcing

                We *are ready to birth*
                                Ourselves.

Here on this wind whipped roof
        comfortable in the knowing
                that the times between *satori*—
those times are the dream,
the illusion, simply the stuff between truths.

And freedom is here, in these slivered parts,
        where there's nothing to offer
                but gratitude
        for this love we can't help but
                        be.

WATERING
THE PLANTS

—

Half the leaves are dead on the rosebush.
I wonder what you do with a rosebush
*   when winter is coming?*

The flowers on the mantel
        bend over exalting
                the same thing that stalks
                        everything.

The curved plant in the macramé is
        limp and shriveling from the root.

The tea-pot-bound vine is another leaf longer.

The moss on the branch is still green

                                                    but

        longing.

THIS LITTLE SLIVER OF PARTICLE-RAY BLISS

The curtains start to breathe when the
light comes in ale from our burning star
that hangs low out there. It doesn't last
long, this little sliver of particle-ray bliss.
The cars go by on their way home.
Everyone thinks about what's for dinner.
I lay on the floor and blow smoke from
the flower into the amber. The cactus in
the tea cup has gummy pink sprouts.
The ceramic stegosaurus is dusty green.
The fabric is cream, knotted and tells
tales when it flutters by the nautilus with
the same shape as the wheel on the Stirling
engine. This happens once when it is
night—unusual for curtains to be awake
so late—while Aristotle and I stir things
with quantum whispers.

IT IS FULL
AGAIN

It is brimming full when I am six and I float
on a houseboat and cousin Jace jumps off the roof.
   Diving, cannon balling, free falling. When I hold
daddy's hand tight through the stalactites and
   stalagmites and screech louder than the bats
when they take off from the dripping rocks and
   soar out over my head. It is full.

The highway stretches over, they call it Cascade
Wonderland. It's my favorite part of the 5 while I am
   fifteen and mama always lets me drive and our two
lanes are empty through the Siskiyous. It is full.

When I come back through, over and over, come
home from college. Come home to visit. Come home
   to stay back home, it's lower every time. Every time
there's more rust colored bank and less
   choppy blue water. Every time.

I go walk at the shore with Uncle Mike one fall,
wandering way down on smooth bank pebbles
    where we all should be submerged.
It's not full now.

Last winter it doesn't snow on Mount Shasta
for the first time in I don't know how many years.
    The Karuk people, they say *it's a sign when
there's no snow on Shasta.*

I drive with Mama and Dawn Marie and before
we stop to take selfies with safari animals, we
    cruise the bridge and here it is getting fuller.

The snow comes down. Eight feet then melts.
Another six. More sun. Over and over all winter
    until the bridge hovers just barely over the water.

And it is full again.

THE SPOT
AT THE CENTER

I tell Aristotle when I touch that place,
that place right there between the breasts
that swells with every breath, where the cage
of life comes together in the middle,
where just under there, everything lives,
I tell him when I touch that place,

This is the best part—on girls and boys.
Right here at the middle, right in between,
at the sternum, I'm not sure why.
But this is the best place.

I bury my nose there where skin
presses against me and hairs fuzz against
the hot breath of my mouth.

LADY
LOVER VINE

The quieter you become
the more you are able to hear.

—Rumi

Some years ago I hear
about this enchanting lover.
I hear she can help you solve your problems.
I hear she can be real jealous. That
she'll show you slithering forest creatures,
screaming jaguars, the most otherworldly
escapes you can scarcely imagine. I hear
to be scared of her. I hear one will be grateful
for her gifts. I hear just about everything
(you know how people like to talk about
the ones who get around).

I almost go to meet her a number of times.
She calls me out to the desert, but I don't go then.
Last summer she calls again. But it isn't until
here, back in the slow, inward depths of winter,
that she and I finally meet. That I finally get
to understand a few things.

You need an introduction to find this
lover—someone who knows how. How to charm
her, how to shape yourself. I hear of a man
who knows her ways. He is full of helpful maps—
he tells me to be patient, he tells me the signs,
where I might find a path, but, he tells me,
it's just between you and her.

The man tells me to prepare and I do all
the things he says, but I don't quite know
why. She's bitter at first taste. Swampy
in my mouth, gritty, acrid, pungent,
so full of her.

The man sings songs and my body rolls.
She softly strokes, rifling through my things,
playing gently—*just who are you, creature?* she
ponders. *Why have you come? How are you ordered?*
What's left to do? Can I make love here?

She touches the places deep that bring me joy.
As she sorts, my heart grows. Bliss fills me, air heavy
with tobacco and sweet with rose water. I still
can't quite see—she is sneaky, shy and curious. But
I feel her brush her hand across my forehead before
I drift off to sleep.

I want more of her when I wake. I want all
of her and feel excitement to journey to
her again. I am nervous about the things
she may find that aren't to her taste.
But I want more.

I return to the man at nightfall for another sip.
I look at the cup, convinced there isn't enough.
I need more, this hungry brain-mind says. I need
more. This will not work. This man, he holds what
I want away from me. This man is just pretending
to help me find her. This man is a problem.
Everything is a problem.

When I lay down with her, she slips further away.
Uninterested in the keepings, she flees off deep
leaving darkness, lonely and excruciating. The
empty space invites the stories she knows she
can provoke. This mind makes so many stories—
bleak, pitiful stories. Anger swells that she has
come and left. This is not what I come here for.
I did so much for you. This. Is. Not. What. I. Want.

But, *dear creature,* she may ask, *What do I want?*
I do not know. I cannot hear.

She finds just then, in my things, a useful game.
I love you. I'm sorry. Please forgive me. Thank you.
Ram Dass calls mantras mind protection. I use
them but never with much consistency. I glimpse
their power but never seize it wholly. *This game
will serve you,* she says. *Play this game.*

I love you. I'm sorry. Please forgive me. Thank you.

Say it, mind. And again. Watch the revulsion. Watch
the boredom. Say it again. She leaves me alone in
the dark while I play my game. *I love you. I'm sorry.
Please forgive me. Thank you. I love you. I'm sorry.
Please forgive me. Thank you.* Long painful hours
drip by. The sharp clatter begins to calm.

In the longest silence a wrenching realization.
My purpose here—I think about asking but don't
in so many words—she simply knows. My purpose
here—every face I am and love flashes before me—
is to love. Fiercely. *Love these humans of yours
fiercely*, she says. *That's your only purpose here.*
I shake and heave from the weight of her truth.
Crying in silent gulps, I return to the game.

I love you. I'm sorry. Please forgive me. Thank you.
How many times should I have rang these sounds?
Perhaps I am repaying some cosmic word debt.
But then I hear her whisper while she still hides:
This is what your soul must hear from your mind.

The servant bucks and pulls.
I love you. I'm sorry. Please forgive me. Thank you.
Rationalizes and reasons.
I love you. I'm sorry. Please forgive me. Thank you.
Screams and cries.
I love you. I'm sorry. Please forgive me. Thank you.
Complains and spews vitriol.
I love you. I'm sorry. Please forgive me. Thank you.
Thrashes relentlessly until everything finally
falls into fitful sleep.

This mysterious beautiful one I seek holds me,
beaten and bruised. But feeling for the first time:

My soul breathes instead of my mind.

She retreats in the light of that third day
while fury remains heavy at my brow.
I love you. I'm sorry. Please forgive me. Thank you.
Fuck. This. I hate this. This is not what I want.
But, *dear creature,* she may ask, *What do I want?*
I do not know. I cannot hear.

I smudge with sage. I chop herbs and cook chicken
with rice and eat, tasting not much of anything.
I love you. I'm sorry. Please forgive me. Thank you.
I sleep more and when I wake I go to the shower.
I shake last night's dread off this body.
Rinse with hot water, scrub with sea salt.
I love you. I'm sorry. Please forgive me. Thank you.

I don't want to trek after her again. But I know
she is waiting. I feel raw and tousled from two
nights' journey. The man lights the tobacco
and prays and I then feel, from the spot at my
center, my own prayers rise.

Dear lady,

I love you. I'm sorry. Please forgive me. Thank you.
I come here humble, seeking only to meet you.
I am full of gratitude for the gifts you give.
I am thankful for this teacher who leads me
       here repeatedly.
I want to understand.
I want to be open and surrender.
I want to trust this process.
Thank you, already, for calming me here tonight.
In all beings highest good, I ask these things.

When I drink for the third time I feel her
even before I swallow. I lay down with her.
I love you. I'm sorry. Please forgive me. Thank you.
I play my game as she desires.
Over and over I chant
to myself,
to her,
to existence,
these potent phrases of surrender:
I love you. I'm sorry. Please forgive me. Thank you.

She smiles and reaches for me in that sacred
spot, deep at the center, where language can't
go. I learn (with nothing short of the flash of an
infant grasping the first word) that the way she
wishes to commune is so swift, vast and intricate
that no mind language can play.

My soul has a language I am clumsy at using.
Maybe it has been fumbled with before—in a
sacred moment with a lover, gasping at the void
of this place I come from. Utter openness. A
boundless network absorbed in all things.

We float in this expanse of charged body jelly,
her and I, swirling, interfacing, intimately wound.
When my mind tries to catch up, only then does
she shy away. I eye the servant sternly,
demanding from it the game.

I love you. I'm sorry. Please forgive me. Thank you.

Silence.

Soul song.

In the silence she keeps coming back to play.
I hear the man still chanting and I finally understand
these love songs that caress and charm and beg—
just for her, everything is for her. This cocoon
dripping in tobacco, silken with surrender. Just
how she likes it. Everywhere, in here, touching in
every space, the bits, staggering in their volume,
exchange.

This is the place, I realize, where I can ask anything.
*How, my love, can I—can I—cultivate many loving
relationships?* It takes more than one try to
ask without words. But then so instantly—
understanding. I understand what it means to be
a lover. I understand that a lover knows their value
and comes forward only in the utmost respect,
understanding one another's terms, coexisting
in a space safe to steep in each other deeply.
I understand that when I prepare for her it is
a love offering to this space,
to our communication,
connection,
relationship.

Life is communication.

I understand that in this soul language, surrendered
wholly, she will generously share whatever is sought.

I'm shy to ask much,
because you don't want to ask too much
from your lover.
I inquire instead,
What, my love, can I give you?
You can have everything.
Everything here that I have,
buried in all of these cells,
all of my stories,
they are yours.
Drink of them deeply,
for you have given me so much.

She keeps sipping until
the spot at my center
is raw and pink and hoarse
from singing a song
it has never sung before.

WE LEARN HOW
BIG WE CAN BE

*You must love in such a way that
the person you love feels free.*

–Thich Nhat Hanh

Back on the first night
I sleep with Chronos, I hear
knuckles rap lightly
on my coup's side-window glass.

Eye crinkles tip-off the smirk
hiding in his helmet as
he pulls beside me at a red on Lincoln
and revs his yellow Kawasaki.

A week later I squeeze the grab handle
in his Lexus as rubber breaks loose on
rain-slicked road and he drifts
the Venice traffic circle.

Downpour sprays up as blue
strobes the sky behind us.
Two rights, a left and the length
of one alley later, we feel safe enough
to inch back toward dinner.

Later between hotel sheets
I press my head hard against his chest
and up under his chin and he sounds like maybe
he's whispering to himself
when he says
I really like you.

Chronos is twenty and I am twenty-four
when he answers my Craigslist ad

    (a nostalgic beg to make-out
    on a couch and play Nintendo)

with this grace and space for me to fall in love
again and again
while I love him.

When I push my head (again) against
that place tonight in bed
he says
This is the part of the day that's the best.

We learn how big we can be,
how much love can fit,
if we let each other be free.

The precise moment I fall in love with him
seven years ago
I am sitting in the passenger seat of the LS400
in the parking lot of the best place
to get breakfast burritos in Pasadena.

WHEN WE ALL
SEE DIFFERENT THINGS

Could a greater miracle take place
than for us to look through
each other's eyes for an instant?

—Henry David Thoreau

In the outside the deck boards are covered with
little lime sprouts fallen from the oak tree.
The fir over there is the oldest thing here and its
tips drip with orange glaze frosting

the pulse in the middle ripples the seams
of this loosely spun fairytale that hangs in the gauze
of the thing
that connects everything.

Almost summer bugs hover in the shimmer of now.
Their wings flicker faster than illusions of a minute
ago or ten.
Inside and outside are two different things
of the same thing
I jump between.

I tingle when the boy Sierra brings
says over and over
I just can't get over
how we can never imagine
what someone else sees.

EVERYDAY (FOR THE PAST THIRTY DAYS)

Yoga is a means of waking up
from our spiritual amnesia,
so that we can remember
all that we already know.

—Donna Fahri

The alarm.
        Seven forty five.
I roll over.
I go turn the clothes back on.
I suck down the water in the blue bottle.
I drop an electrolyte tab in to fizz and
        lay down on the floor until the dryer buzz.
The armload of laundry is warm when Aristotle
        picks it up from where I toss it and piles it
        back on top of me.

He goes to change his shorts.
I fold my Pendleton towel.
     The black shower towel.
        The Lycra sports bra.
           The white and black trunks.
I roll a tiger print mat and gulp
     the bubbling pink.
My bag is burlap, mat up to one side,
     shampoo and conditioner floating
        down there.
Towels and clothes to the other,
     my canteen.
I always back out of the driveway slow.
Flip a U.
     Right on 102nd.
     Take the rounding ramp
        on to Halsey over to Fremont Street.

I go to the studio everyday.
I leave my shoes at the foot of the stairs.
        His tucked neatly. Mine haphazard.

              In the mirrored room
                we pick our place.

Half done, just when we want to die—face red,
        sweat dripping—we watch ourselves
        standing there like trees.
Grow like trees we hear.

                The forest drips
                in the quiet room.
                From his elbows.
                  My thighs.
                These trees.

ON MY
WAY HERE

A stranger walks down the sidewalk, pretty
sarong, all noble in reds. Every fabric that swaths
her looks of the hand that weaves it, dyes it, sews
it. Hair golden wild, brushed by sleep and sunshine.
Tan over shadows of triceps and trim pelvic bones.
Alighting barefoot on the cement, soft steps,
purposeful motion pushing that baby stroller.

I expect her baby to be (just as he is) steeped
in this mother and our Mother alike. Planted strong
in this that grows us, she plods about with enough
sense to know where she comes from, even while
navigating this strange paved way through hardware
stores and traffic lights. I want to be like this.
But I am driving.

This stranger invites me to remember that
I live forever in the bask of two summers ago
when us sacred seven get lost in ancient trees
and fall over counting how many greens and
untie our sneakers to let mud in between
our toes. We roll down grassy hills and believe
this circle will be our people forever.

Sierra and I listen to secrets of conifer seeds
and I scour the floor to weave a nest the size
of my outstretched arms. Love holds her crystal
ball but we don't care about the future and when
dry twigs crackle and my woven altar is blazed,
burgeoning, Mother knows we are here from the
fire tornado.

A LITTLE ASTONISHMENT
GOES A LONG WAY

A crab appears skittering wildly;
     fast, focused.
I watch with intrigue at this little instrument of
     wild—
a piece of seaweed clings slimy and dark green
     to its hind.
The sand grooves with its dance.
     It seems aloof until it is certainly
coming to me and stops at my feet.

Taken aback I draw my toes in close
and jump when I hear
     I can't hurt you.

It speaks.

I can't hurt you because you have a hard shell like me.

We're kindred.

I can't hurt you because in your windy paths you think
you don't know where you're going.
But you're getting there.
Sideways.

We're kindred.

I can't hurt you because you're so big.
Don't you know how big you are?

We're kindred.

I am the whole sea. And so are you.

We're kindred.

I SPIN
THROUGH

———

There is a sailboat out there at sea.
Just in the glistening patch.
There is a jungle behind me
        after a stretch of sea grass.
There is a dune that I climb and from that perch
        I watch the horizon in every direction—
                my ring of solitude, oneness, fullness
                        around.

As I spin
        faster and faster
                time speeds up with me.

And it is day and it is starry and it is light again and
the moon came and went and the seasons too and
I spin through year after turn until the joy of my
dervish throws me flat on my back and the rattle
of my existence shakes without mercy.

There exploding again

I feel this tough crab shell break.

        A crack
where there wasn't such tenderness before.

I roll down my hill head over feet and spring into
a leap, burst into a run, and fling everything away
until my goose pimpled flesh is the only thing
between me and sea foam.

Ankle deep,
        knee deep,
                hip bones,
                        a sharp gasp at the cold.

                My Mother baptizes me
                and welcomes me home.

THEY SAY
IT IS A SACRED SPACE

I always think it is beautiful then—
the big arches, the wooden planked ceiling,
the long benches. The place I sing hymns.

My kindergarten teacher stands up in front there
and says with the same conviction
that she names the colors
that one day (we just don't know which one)
we'll all rise up out of here, out of our clothes,
through the pretty wood ceiling,
up to heaven to be with god.

I always think it is beautiful there.
Until I watch my daddy confess his sins, crying,
then dipped clean, still not sure he is whole.
Until I watch mama go kneel before that god
who hasn't taken me yet, sobbing, surrendered,
broken. The frail old lady behind me
has a perfect silver updo and her voice
sings soprano. *Holy. Holy. Holy is the Lord God
Almighty.* The man is red faced while he yells
about the ways I should be.

They say it is a sacred space.

I roll out my afghan and light
a dollar store Jesus candle.
When I burn the palo santo
this place is sacred.
When the spot in the center cracks open raw
my grandmother's grandmother's great-
grandmother sings with me,

Remember sweet child, remember you're okay,
and you're the whole thing.

Everything here is for you
to remember—

You made it just for you
to remember—

When you die you return to
read these words you forgot you wrote
to remind you that you've forgotten
everything.

Remember—

you're love

and nothing else.

BETWEEN ME
AND THE STUCCO

———

Five planets are in retrograde,
it's Love's nameday and the one
I want to love is out of town today.

It's hot outside and stuffy in here.
When I burn a full page of scrawl
on a yellow legal pad, smoke
tendrils up from an abalone shell.

Between me and the stucco
light years unravel.

I remember again
how many times
I've been

but

never

quite like this.

Ash Good was born in Paradise, California, and raised in a small Oregon mill town. She is the author of *Years Grew a Keloid* and studied design and art history in Los Angeles at Loyola Marymount University. Ash holds sacred space to invite all beings to connect with their healer and artist within. She lives in Portland, Oregon.

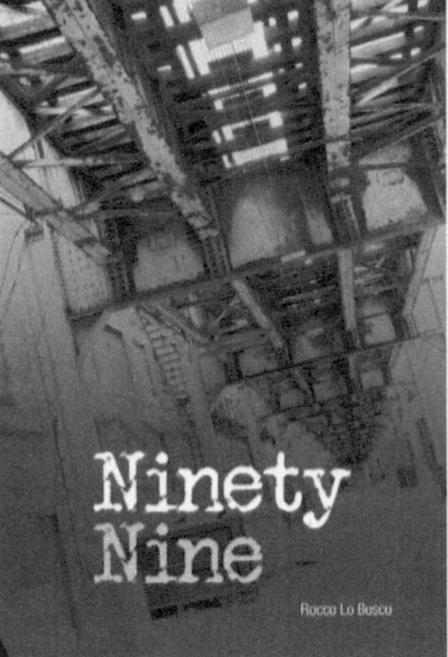

Forthcoming...

Michael Ventura's
*From These Tenements
Rise Visions* (2017)

The Complete Works
of Jo Carol Pierce (TBA)

Guy Juke's *The Poetry of
Blackie White* (TBA)

LETTERSAT
3AMPRESS